MW01047378

Eli's Owie and the Butterfly Kiss

Words and Pictures by Marianne Hegg

This book is dedicated to my children,
Ronin, Robert and Pamela

Marianne lives with her husband, three children, one dog and a turtle! She has a treasure trove of stories to tell. When she is not writing books, you can ususally find her outside enjoying her home in The Pacific Northwest or hanging out with her family Big Sky Montana.

If you enjoy this book, please leave a review. Thank you!

Eli's Owie and the Butterfly Kiss

Words and Pictures by Marianne Hegg

Copyright © 2020 by Mariane Hegg
Book Design by Sandra Moreano
All rights reserved
ISBN: 9781670825926

Eli the elephant went on
a walk in a great green jungle.

OH NO!

He bumped his
Trunk!

OUCH!

It hurt!

He went to search
for help.

He looked up in the tree.
What did he see?

It was Monkey and his friend.
They could not help.

They were too busy juggling
yellow bananas!

What was that in the water?

It was Hippo!

Oh no!
She couldn't help him either.

She was too busy blowing bubbles in the blue water.

Eli kept on
walking.

It looked
like something was
hiding in the grass.

Maybe it could
help make his
owie better.

It was Tiger!
But he was too busy
counting his black and
orange stripes!

Eli wouldn't give up.

He sees something
by the river...

It was Crocodile!
Oh no! He couldn't help.
He was too busy
brushing his sharp,
white teeth.

Wait. Was that just
rocks over there?

He went to take
a closer look.

They were turtles! Oh boy!
They were too busy playing a
game of freeze tag!

Eli sat down. Maybe everyone was too busy to help make his owie better.

Just then, a special friend flew by...

It was...

...Butterfly!

"I can help," she said!

Then she kissed his owie
and made it better!

That's when Eli learned
that butterfly kisses
were the *best* kisses!